NECESSARY NUTRIENTS

Fats as Necessary Nutrients

BY KIMBERLY ZIEMANN

Kids Core
An Imprint of Abdo Publishing
abdobooks.com

abdobooks.com

Published by Abdo Publishing, a division of ABDO, PO Box 398166, Minneapolis, Minnesota 55439. Copyright © 2023 by Abdo Consulting Group, Inc. International copyrights reserved in all countries. No part of this book may be reproduced in any form without written permission from the publisher. Kids Core™ is a trademark and logo of Abdo Publishing.

Printed in the United States of America, North Mankato, Minnesota.
102022
012023

Cover Photo: Shutterstock Images
Interior Photos: Wavebreak Media/Shutterstock Images, 4–5, 10–11; iStockphoto, 6, 25 (right); T. A. McKay/iStockphoto, 8; Dmytro Zinkevych/Shutterstock Images, 12; Shutterstock Images, 13, 16, 22, 24, 28 (bottom), 29 (top), 29 (bottom); Miaden Zivkovic/iStockphoto, 14; Prostock Studio/Shutterstock Images, 18–19; Dragon Images/Shutterstock Images, 20; Marie C. Fields/Shutterstock Images, 25 (left); Sergii Koval/Shutterstock Images, 26; Elena Shashkina/Shutterstock, 28 (top)

Editor: Ann Schwab
Series Designer: Layna Darling

Library of Congress Control Number: 2022940678

Publisher's Cataloging-in-Publication Data

Names: Ziemann, Kimberly, author.
Title: Fats as necessary nutrients / by Kimberly Ziemann
Description: Minneapolis, Minnesota: Abdo Publishing, 2023 | Series: Necessary nutrients | Includes online resources and index.
Identifiers: ISBN 9781098290023 (lib. bdg.) | ISBN 9781098275228 (ebook)
Subjects: LCSH: Oils and fats--Juvenile literature. | Lipids--Metabolism--Juvenile literature. | Lipids in human nutrition--Juvenile literature. | Nutrition--Health aspects--Juvenile literature.
Classification: DDC 613.2--dc23

CONTENTS

CHAPTER 1
What Are Fats? 4

CHAPTER 2
Why Are Fats Important? 10

CHAPTER 3
Choosing Healthy Fats 18

Nutrient Jobs 28
Glossary 30
Online Resources 31
Learn More 31
Index 32
About the Author 32

After a busy day at school, many kids look forward to having a snack.

CHAPTER 1

What Are Fats?

Tyler arrives home from school. He has homework to do before dinner. But it's been a long day. He's hungry and tired. He needs to find an energy boost. Tyler steps into the kitchen for a snack.

In addition to healthy fats, almonds are full of protein, fiber, vitamins, and minerals.

A chocolate cookie would taste good. But it wouldn't give him energy for long. He grabs a handful of almonds instead. The fats in this healthy snack will keep him full until dinner. The almonds will also give him energy so he can focus on his homework.

Fats in Foods

Cookies and nuts both have fats. But they have different types of fats. The kind of fats a person eats matters. Fats are **nutrients**. Nutrients are things needed for the body to grow and stay alive. Fats give the body energy to work properly.

There are three basic types of fats. Food can have saturated, unsaturated, or trans fats. Some fats are healthier than others. Almonds have lots of unsaturated fats. This is the healthiest type of fat. Cookies have more saturated fats.

Cookies and other baked goods often contain trans fats.

Forms of Fats

Saturated fats are usually solid at room temperature. Butter is a saturated fat. Unsaturated fats are liquid at room temperature. Olive oil is an unsaturated fat.

Some cookies might also contain trans fats. Saturated and trans fats are less healthy types of fats.

The human body needs some fats to work right. These are **essential** fats. They can't be made by the body. Choosing foods with healthy fats helps keep the body working well.

Explore Online

Visit the website below. Does it give you any new information about fats that wasn't in Chapter One?

Learning about Fats

abdocorelibrary.com/fats-as -necessary-nutrients

Healthy fats provide essential nutrients needed for growth and development.

CHAPTER 2

Why Are Fats Important?

The human body uses fats in many ways. Fats are important building blocks for the body's **cells**. They provide energy to fuel the body. Healthy fats help brains develop and bodies grow.

Some of the energy fats provide is used by the body right after eating.

Stored fats help keep internal organs safe from injury.

When people eat fats, some are used right away as energy. Excess amounts are stored inside the cells for later use. Children use more fats for energy than adults. Infants between nine and fifteen months burn twice as much energy as adults. It is very important they have enough healthy fats in their diet. If this doesn't happen, it may harm their growth.

Carrots are rich in vitamin A. They also supply the body with vitamin C, calcium, iron, and other nutrients.

Helping the Body

Fats do more than provide energy and help bodies grow. Stored fat cushions and protects the heart, kidneys, and other organs. Fat also **insulates** the body to keep it at the right temperature.

Fats are important in other ways too. Fats help the body absorb and store important nutrients. All minerals and many vitamins dissolve in water. But the vitamins A, D, E, and K do not. Foods containing these vitamins need to be eaten with fats so the body can use them. These vitamins are found in foods such as carrots, spinach, and sweet potatoes.

Lipids

Fats are a type of lipid. Lipids include fats, oils, and waxes. There are thousands of different lipids in the body. Their most important role is to provide energy for the body. High levels of some lipids can cause harm.

Eating fish such as salmon helps the body feel full after a meal.

Fats are **digested** slowly. Eating foods that contain fats helps people feel full. This helps them avoid overeating. Not eating enough healthy fats can make people feel hungry all the time. It is important to eat the right amount of fats each day.

Primary Source

A study led by researcher John C. Kostyak found that children burn more body fat than adults. Kostyak said:

> [Enough] fat must be included in the diet for children to support normal growth and development.

Source: "Kids Burn More Fat, and Need More Fat, Than Adults." *Reuters*, 28 Aug. 2007, reuters.com. Accessed 12 Mar. 2022.

Comparing Texts

Think about the quote. Does it support the information in this chapter? Or does it give a different perspective? Explain how in a few sentences.

Using olive oil in salad dressings is a good way to include healthy fats in a person's diet.

CHAPTER 3

Choosing Healthy Fats

Children ages 4 to 18 should get 25 to 35 percent of their daily **calories** from fats. Some fats are better for the body than others. People can keep their bodies working well by eating mostly healthy fats.

Because most ice cream contains a high amount of saturated fats, it is best enjoyed occasionally.

Saturated and Trans Fats

Saturated fats and trans fats are unhealthy when eaten too often. Too much of these fats can lead to illness and weight gain. They can also increase the risk of many diseases. These diseases can affect the heart, brain, and other organs in the body.

Saturated fats are usually in foods that come from animals. Beef, pork, and ice cream are examples of these foods. Many baked goods, like brownies and cake, have this type of fat too. Less than 10 percent of calories should come from saturated fats.

Trans fats are mostly from vegetable oils that have been processed. These oils have been changed to be more solid at room temperature.

Donuts and other fried foods often have trans fats.

Fried foods such as french fries and fried chicken often have trans fats. Some cookies, pizzas, and donuts may also have trans fats. It is best to eat as little trans fat as possible.

A Healthier Choice

Unsaturated fats are healthier fats. Fats contain smaller parts called fatty acids. The fatty acids in unsaturated fats are nutrients that the body needs to work right. Unsaturated fats come mostly from plants. There are two types of this fat.

Mega Nutrition

Two of the essential fatty acids in unsaturated fats are omega-3 fatty acids and omega-6 fatty acids. The body cannot make these nutrients, so they must be eaten. Some foods containing omega-3 fatty acids are fish, walnuts, flaxseeds, and canola oil. Omega-6 fatty acids can be found in sunflower seeds, tofu, and almonds.

Avocados are a popular source of monounsaturated fats.

　　Monounsaturated fats are found in avocados, olives, and some nuts and seeds. Polyunsaturated fats are often found in fish. Good sources are salmon, trout, and sardines.

Comparing Fats

Sugar Cookie

Serving size:	One 3-inch (8-cm) cookie
Calories	139
Fat content	
Saturated fat	2.3g
Monounsaturated fat	2.1g
Polyunsaturated fat	1.1g

Almonds

Serving size:	23 almonds
Calories	160
Fat content	
Saturated fat	1g
Monounsaturated fat	9g
Polyunsaturated fat	3.5g

Source: USDA.gov

Here are the nutritional details for sugar cookies and almonds. Compare and contrast the amounts of saturated fat and unsaturated fat in each one. Polyunsaturated fats and monounsaturated fats are both types of unsaturated fats. Add their numbers together to get the total grams of unsaturated fats. Which snack would be a healthier choice?

Chia seeds are often made into healthy puddings. They are also used in smoothie bowls or sprinkled on top of salads.

It can also be found in canola oil, flaxseeds, and chia seeds.

People do not have to give up all the foods they love to be healthy. Enjoying smaller amounts of foods considered less healthy is okay! But most meals should have unsaturated fats. Essential fats are a necessary nutrient in a well-balanced diet.

Further Evidence

Look at the website below. Does it give any new evidence to support Chapter Three?

Rethink Fats

abdocorelibrary.com/fats-as -necessary-nutrients

Nutrient Jobs

Fats give the body energy.

Fats help the body absorb vitamins.

Fats help the body grow.

Eating foods that contain fats helps keep people full and avoid overeating.

Glossary

calories
units for measuring the amount of energy food makes when eaten

cells
the smallest and most basic units of life

digested
broken-down food and liquids absorbed by the body

essential
something that is necessary or required

insulates
covers to prevent the loss of heat

nutrient
a substance needed for the body's health

Online Resources

To learn more about fats as necessary nutrients, visit our free resource websites below.

Visit **abdocorelibrary.com** or scan this QR code for free Common Core resources for teachers and students, including vetted activities, multimedia, and booklinks, for deeper subject comprehension.

Visit **abdobooklinks.com** or scan this QR code for free additional online weblinks for further learning. These links are routinely monitored and updated to provide the most current information available.

Learn More

Shapiro, Nina L. *The Ultimate Kids' Guide to Being Super Healthy*. Sky Pony, 2021.

Stevens, Jamaica. *The Vegetarian Cookbook for Kids*. Rockridge, 2021.

Index

calories, 19, 21, 25

energy, 5–7, 11, 13–15

fatty acids, 23

lipid, 15

monounsaturated fat, 24–25

nutrient, 7, 15, 23, 27

polyunsaturated fat, 24–25

saturated fats, 7–9, 21, 25

trans fat, 7, 9, 21–22

unsaturated fat, 7–8, 23, 25, 27

About the Author

Kimberly Ziemann lives in Nebraska with her husband and three daughters. She works as a reading teacher with elementary students. While she enjoys writing books for children, her favorite activity is reading. She also loves playing with her two dogs and snuggling with her cat.